LiTTLE RED RiDiNG HOOD

as told by
Mabel Watts

illustrated by
Kelly Oechsli

© COPYRIGHT 1965 BY WESTERN PUBLISHING COMPANY, INC.

WHITMAN PUBLISHING COMPANY

RACINE, WISCONSIN

Printed in the U.S.A. by Western Printing and Lithographing Company

Many long summers ago there was a little girl whose mother made her a red cape with a hood for her birthday.

She wore it here, there, and everywhere because it was so pretty. And that's why everyone called her Little Red Riding Hood.

One morning Mr. Whittle, the woodcutter, called at Little Red Riding
Hood's cottage in the woods.

"Your grandmother is sick," he said,
"and lonesome."

"May I take a basket of goodies to her?"
Little Red Riding Hood asked her mother.

"That would cheer her," agreed Mother. "It would make her feel better."

Mother put some cookies and some butter rolls and some fresh elderberry jam into a basket.

Little Red Riding Hood added a bag of colored jelly beans.

Then she put on her cape and kissed her mother good-bye.

"Keep to the path, child," said Mother. "Don't loiter along the way. And don't talk to strangers."

"I'll do just as you say," promised Little Red Riding Hood.

And off she trotted, with the basket on her arm, her red cape flying in the breeze.

The birds sang merrily as Little Red Riding Hood walked through the shadowy woods. Bunnies chased. Squirrels scampered. And the fawns peeped shyly from among the trees.

"Good morning, friends," said Little Red Riding Hood. "But I can't stop and play with you today!"

She pulled her hood over her head, and
sang:
"Here I go to Grandma's house,
To Grandma's house I go!"

"Ho! Ho!" said a gruff, growly voice. "So *that's* where you're going!" And a great, gray wolf pounced out from behind a blackberry bush.

"Please let me pass," said Little Red Riding Hood. "I must hurry!"

The wolf peeped into the basket. "MM-mm," he said. "All my favorites!"

"All *Grandma's* favorites!" said Little Red Riding Hood. "Oh, please move aside."

"Wait a minute," said the wolf, becoming friendly. "Why not pick some flowers for your Grandmother?"

"Well-ll," said Little Red Riding Hood.
"I really shouldn't stop!"

"A few minutes won't make any differ-
ence," said the wolf.

So Little Red Riding Hood stopped to
pick some bluebells and buttercups.

And when she was finished and looked
up, the wolf was gone.

He was bounding along to Grandmother's house. "Here's the place," he said.
And he knock-knock-knocked on the door.

"Who is there?" asked Grandmother.
"It's Little Red Riding Hood," called
the wolf, in a little-girl voice. "I've brought
you some goodies to make you well."

"Bless your heart!"
said Grandmother.
"Come in, dear!"
The wolf lifted
the latch and
laughed, "Boo!"

Grandmother hopped out of bed and slipped through the open door.

Zip, she went, through the cabbage patch. *Zip,* through the woods.

After she had gone the wicked wolf popped into a nightgown and a nightcap.

He put on Grandmother's spectacles and climbed into bed.

"Now I look a little *less* like a wolf," he said, "and just a little *more* like Grandmother!"

Soon there was a knock on the door.

"Lift the latch, dear, and come in," called the wolf in Grandmother's voice.

Little Red Riding Hood hurried inside.

"Why, Grandma," she said, "what long, furry ears you have!"

"All the better to hear you, my dear," said the wolf cheerfully.

"And your eyes!" said Little Red Riding Hood. "Oh, my! They look like big, green marbles!"

"All the better to see you, my dear!" said the wolf.

"My, oh, my, Grandma," said Little Red Riding Hood, "what long, jagged teeth you have!"

The wily, wicked wolf smacked his chops. "All the better to EAT you!" he snapped, and he jumped out of bed.

But Little Red Riding Hood was quick.
She skipped and hopped and ran around
the room until the wolf was dizzy.

Then she ran through the door —
straight into the arms of Mr. Whittle, the
woodcutter. "The wolf is after me!" cried
Little Red Riding Hood.

"And we are after *him*!" replied Grandmother, for she was there, too.

"You'll be sorry!" Mr. Whittle told the
wolf. "Now it's your turn to be afraid."

The wolf ran and yelped and ran, like
a big coward — with the woodcutter right
after him, swinging his ax.

"Everything's going to be all right now," Grandmother told Little Red Riding Hood.

And that's exactly how things turned out!

The woodcutter was soon back — all
alone. "No more trouble!" he said. "No
more wolf!"

"Hurray!" said Little Red Riding Hood.

"Thank goodness!" said Grandmother.
"Now we can live in peace and quiet!"

Then all three sat down to enjoy the goodies in Little Red Riding Hood's basket — the cookies, the butter rolls, the elderberry jam, and the jelly beans. It was just like a party!